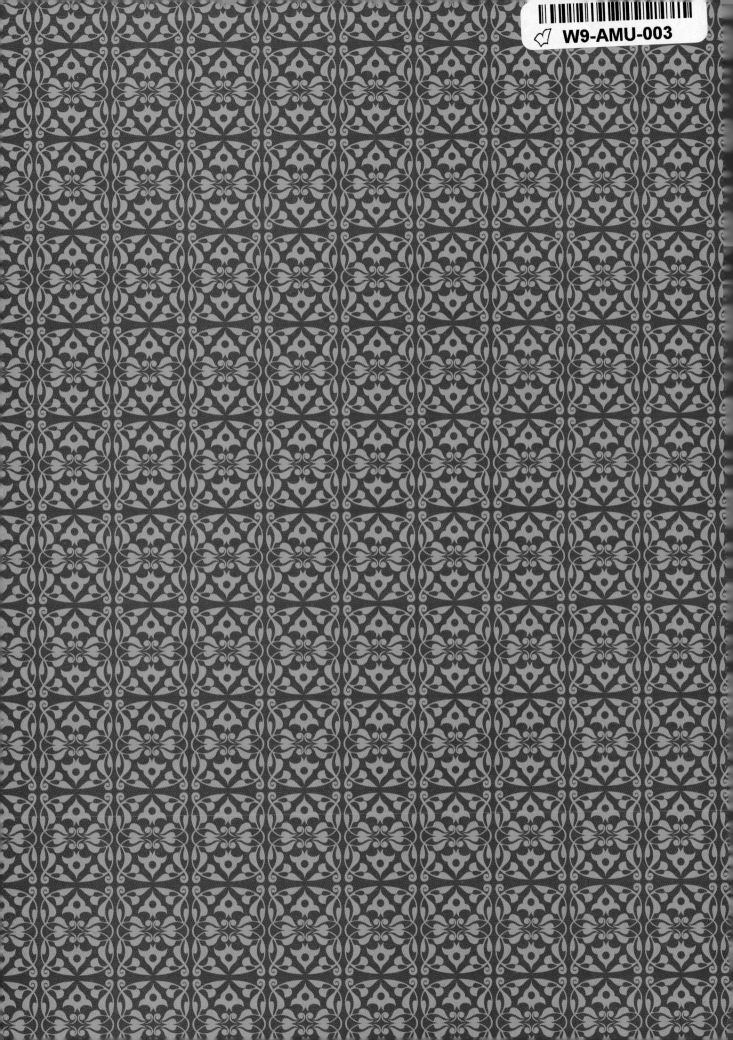

C L A S S I C
BEDTIME
S T O R I E S

PUBLICATIONS INTERNATIONAL, LTD.

Title page illustrated by Robin Moro

Cover illustrated by David Grasso

Louis Weber, C.E.O.

Publications International, Ltd.

7373 North Cicero Avenue

Lincolnwood, Illinois 60646

Manufactured in China.

8 7 6 5 4 3 2 1

ISBN: 0-7853-2700-2

CONTENTS

⚜

The Nightingale *4*

The Brave Little Tailor *20*

Demeter and Persephone *32*

Gulliver's Travels *46*

Ali Baba *60*

The Five Brothers *74*

The Nightingale

Adapted by Lisa Harkrader
Illustrated by Robin Moro

Many years ago, the emperor of China lived in a palace that was surrounded by beautiful gardens. Visitors came from all over the world to admire his silk draperies, exquisite vases, and rare flowers.

But after the visitors toured the palace and gardens, they wanted to see more. "Don't let our trip end," they would say.

A fisherman heard these words. "I can show you the most beautiful thing in all of China," he would say.

He began leading visitors into the forest to see a beautiful nightingale that lived there. At first the visitors would grumble. "We trudged all the way out here to see a plain gray bird?"

But then the nightingale would open its mouth. Its voice was pure and strong. Its song was lovelier than anything the visitors had ever heard.

The visitors returned home and told their friends about the nightingale's beautiful singing. More people came to visit the palace, the gardens, and the plain gray bird that sang in the forest. The nightingale became known as the most beautiful thing in all of China. Everyone had heard of this remarkable bird.

Everyone, that is, except the emperor himself.

The emperor of China was an old man. He stayed inside his palace and knew nothing of the nightingale's lovely song.

One day the emperor of China received a letter that came from the emperor of Japan.

"I have heard of your wonderful nightingale," the Japanese emperor wrote. "He is the most beautiful thing in all of China. Some people say he is the most beautiful thing in all the world. I will arrive in two days to pay you a visit and admire this heavenly bird."

The emperor of China was puzzled. He summoned his prime minister. "Have you heard of this nightingale that is the most beautiful thing in all of China?" the emperor asked.

"No, Your Excellency." The prime minister scratched his chin. "Your painted screens, or your silver chimes, or your delicate orchids could be the most beautiful things in China. But nightingales are quite plain."

"That may be," said the emperor. "But the emperor of Japan arrives in two days. He expects to see this nightingale. Search until you find it."

The prime minister started in the cellar and ended in the attic. He looked under rugs and behind furniture. He searched every inch of the palace, but he could not find the nightingale.

Now there was only one day left before the Japanese emperor's arrival. The emperor of China was worried. He summoned the prime minister and all the palace guards.

"The emperor of Japan will be here tomorrow," the Chinese emperor told them. "He is expecting to see this nightingale that is the most beautiful thing in all of China. Spread out and search the gardens. The bird must be there somewhere."

The prime minister and the palace guards trooped out into the gardens. They climbed trees and waded through fountains. They turned over rocks and peeked under shrubs. They searched every inch of every garden, but they could not find the nightingale.

The next morning the emperor of China received a message. The Japanese emperor's ship had just sailed into the harbor. The Chinese emperor summoned the prime minister, the palace guards, and all the lords and ladies of the court.

"The emperor of Japan will be here today," he told them. "Spread out into the forest surrounding my gardens. Don't come back until you've found this magnificent nightingale."

The prime minister, the palace guards, and all the lords and ladies of the court trekked into the woods. They shook vines and rustled leaves. They peeked in hollow logs and splashed through streams.

They were about to give up when they came upon the fisherman. He led them to the nightingale.

The prime minister, followed by the guards and all the lords and ladies of the court, marched into the palace as the Japanese emperor arrived.

"So this is the famous nightingale, the most beautiful thing in all of China," said the emperor of Japan. "I must say, he looks rather plain."

The nightingale flew to the windowsill. He opened his mouth. Out came the most beautiful song either of the emperors had ever heard. The emperor of Japan was speechless. The emperor of China cried tears of joy.

The nightingale warbled and trilled until even the prime minister, the palace guards, and all the lords and ladies of the court were weeping.

"I must find a way to thank you for allowing me to hear your nightingale's song," declared the emperor of Japan. "He truly is the most beautiful thing in all of China."

Day after day the nightingale's song filled the palace. Day after day the people crowded in to hear beautiful music. Day after day someone always said, "Too bad the plain nightingale doesn't look as lovely as he sounds."

The emperor heard these comments, which made him very angry. The nightingale's song had brought him such joy. He was happier now than he had ever been. "I will not have people saying unkind words about the nightingale," he said.

The emperor gave the nightingale a golden perch to sit on. He adorned the nightingale with ribbons and jewels.

The people were delighted. "Now the nightingale looks almost as lovely as he sounds," they said.

Day after day the nightingale sat on his golden perch, wearing his jewels and singing his song. The emperor thought the little bird looked tired and a little sad.

At night the emperor invited the nightingale into his private chambers. There were no golden perches or crowds of people. The nightingale perched on the emperor's bed and sang just for the emperor.

"Gold and ribbons and jewels do not enhance your lovely voice," said the emperor. "You are the most beautiful thing in all of China when you are yourself, singing your pure, sweet song."

The emperor drifted off to sleep each night to the sound of the nightingale's pure, sweet song.

One day a messenger arrived with a present from the emperor of Japan. "I hope you enjoy this gift," wrote the Japanese emperor. "It is a small token compared to the great joy you gave me when you allowed me to listen to the nightingale."

The Chinese emperor opened the package. Inside was a replica of the nightingale, encrusted with emeralds, sapphires, and rubies. On its back was a delicately carved key.

The emperor wound the key. The mechanical bird began to sing one of the nightingale's songs. The bird did not sound quite as lovely as the real nightingale, and it only sang one song, over and over. Still, the emperor was pleased.

He ordered a second golden perch to be placed beside the first. "Now you will get some rest," he told the nightingale.

The people were thrilled. "Finally!" they said. "A nightingale that looks as lovely as it sounds."

They didn't notice that the jeweled bird's song was not as sweet as the real nightingale's song. They asked to hear the new nightingale over and over. The people ignored the real nightingale, so he flew home to the forest.

Only one person noticed that the nightingale had gone—the emperor. He missed his friend deeply.

"Perhaps it's for the best," the emperor said. "The nightingale was unhappy singing for crowds of people day after day. He will be happier in the forest."

The people never grew tired of the mechanical bird's song. The emperor closed his eyes and tried to pretend he was hearing the song of the real nightingale.

The mechanical bird played over and over, day after day, until one morning, with a loud twang and a pop, it stopped.

The emperor shook the bird. The prime minister wriggled its key. The bird would not play. They called in the watchmaker.

"A sprung spring," the watchmaker proclaimed. "I'll fix it, but you'll have to handle the bird with care. Only wind it on special occasions."

The emperor was miserable. He'd lost his friend the nightingale, and now he didn't have the mechanical bird to take his place. The emperor grew sick and weak.

The prime minister, the palace guards, and all the lords and ladies of the court tried everything, but nothing could cure the emperor. The old fisherman heard of the emperor's illness and promptly told the nightingale.

The nightingale flew straight to the emperor's chambers. He perched on his bed and began to sing his beautiful song.

The emperor opened his eyes. "You came back," he whispered. Tears of joy streamed down the emperor's cheeks.

The nightingale sang a sweet song for the emperor. Then the two old friends talked late into the night. The emperor sat up in bed and the color returned to his cheeks.

The nightingale loved the emperor because the emperor appreciated him just as he was. The emperor loved the nightingale because the emperor could be honest with him. All day long the prime minister, the palace guards, and all the lords and ladies of the court told the emperor only what they thought he wanted to hear. But in the evenings, the little nightingale only listened and sang.

"It's because of you that I'm feeling better," said the emperor. "Precious jewels cannot match the beauty of your song, and mechanical parts cannot give the friendship that comes from your heart."

From then on, the nightingale freely roamed the forest during the day. Then at night, he sang his beautiful song to the emperor, making him well and lulling him to sleep.

The Brave Little Tailor

Adapted by Jennifer Boudart
Illustrated by Jeremy Tugeau

One morning, a little tailor sat in his shop. He bent over his work, sewing as he always did this time of day. Suddenly the tailor had a taste for jelly. He took out a loaf of bread, and cut a big slice from it. The tailor licked his lips as he spread on some jelly. "I am more hungry than I thought," he told himself. "Let's hope this jelly fills my belly and clears my head."

The tailor wanted to sew a few more stitches before eating his snack. When he finished, he saw a swarm of flies buzzing around his tasty jelly. The little man waved the flies away with his hand. But they flew right back.

The tailor grabbed a scrap of cloth and growled, "Now I'll let you have it!" The cloth burst through the air as the tailor beat at the buzzing flies.

When he lifted the cloth away, seven flies lay dead on the table. "The whole world should know of my skill!" said the tailor. He cut a belt just his size. With his finest thread, he sewed these words: "Seven in one blow!" The tailor tied the red belt around his waist. "I feel the need for a big adventure," he shouted.

The tailor looked for something useful to take with him on his big adventure. All he found was an old piece of cheese. He put it in his pocket. As he was locking the door, he heard a rustle in the bushes. A bird was trapped among the thorns. The tailor gently pulled the bird from the bush. He put it in his pocket with the cheese. Then he began his adventure.

The tailor walked through town and up the side of a mountain without stopping. At the top, he met a giant. "Hello, Giant," said the tailor with a bow. "I am on a big adventure. Will you join me?"

"A little man like you on a big adventure?" rumbled the giant. For an answer, the tailor showed the giant his belt. The giant read the words: "Seven in one blow!"

The giant found it very hard to believe that this tiny tailor could kill seven men with one blow. So he decided to test the little man's strength. "Can you do this?" asked the giant. He picked up a stone and squeezed it until water dripped from the stone.

"Watch this," the tailor said as he took something from his pocket. The giant thought it was a stone, too, but it was actually the piece of cheese. The tailor squeezed it until liquid whey dripped from his hand.

The giant raised his eyebrows. "Well, can you do this?" he asked. He picked up another stone and tossed it high into the air. It flew almost out of sight.

"Watch this," the tailor said as he took something from his pocket. It was the bird, of course. With a toss of his hand, the tailor sent the little bird flying out of sight.

The giant was a poor loser. "Perhaps you would like to come home with me and meet my friends," the giant said with an evil gleam in his eye.

"Certainly," the tailor replied.

The giant took the tailor to his cave. A group of giants sat around a roaring fire. They watched as their friend lead the little man to a bed. "You can sleep here," said the giant. "Even a man who can kill seven in one blow needs to rest!"

The tailor was not used to such a big bed. So he slept in a corner instead. It was good for him that he did. During the night, the giants pounded on the bed with clubs, until they thought they had taken care of the pesky tailor.

In the morning, the giants went swimming in the river. They joked about the strange man and his silly belt. When the tailor walked up whistling a merry tune, the giants were so afraid, they ran away without their clothes! The tailor laughed and left the giants behind. He walked very far and then lay down for a nap on a soft, grassy hill.

The tailor slept a long time. Some people found him and read his belt. They thought he was a mighty soldier. When the tailor awoke, the people took him to meet their king.

The king had never met a man who could kill seven in one blow. He hired the stranger for his army, and gave him a bag full of gold.

The other soldiers were very angry. "This is not fair, Your Highness! We will leave your army if we don't get a bag full of gold, too."

The king could not lose a whole army over one man. He decided to get rid of his new soldier. So he went to the little man with a challenge. "I need you to kill two giants that live in my woods. If you do, I will give you my daughter and half my kingdom as a reward." The tailor knew this was his chance to become a hero.

The tailor went into the woods the next morning. One hundred soldiers went with him. As he rode, the tailor made a plan. "Stay behind until I call you," he told the soldiers.

Then he rode on until he found the two giants asleep under a tree. The tailor climbed the tree. He began dropping acorns on one giant's head. The giant awoke and turned to his friend. "Why did you wake me by thumping my head?" roared the giant. Before his friend could answer, the angry giant threw an acorn at him.

The two giants fought each other until both fell dead to the ground. The tailor called the king's soldiers to come and see what he had done. They were amazed. The new soldier had beaten the giants without getting a scratch! "Two giants are easy compared to killing seven in one blow," laughed the tailor.

The king heard about the tailor's great feat, but he was not ready to give up his daughter and half his riches, yet. So he thought of a plan. "Brave soldier, a wild boar is tearing up the farmers' crops," explained the king. "Please catch it for me."

Off the tailor went to find the boar. He was not sure how he would catch it, but he knew he would think of something. Suddenly he heard a snort behind him. The boar was coming his way! The tailor ran into a barn. The boar was close behind. The little man crawled out a window just as the boar came through the doors. The tailor ran to shut the doors. The animal was trapped!

When the king asked how he had tricked the beast, the tailor said, "One who can kill seven in one blow can surely get a silly boar to do what he wants!"

The king tried one last trick to get rid of the tailor. He ordered the little man to catch a unicorn that was scaring the villagers. The tailor agreed to go, but only if he could go alone. The king agreed. So the tailor walked into the woods, looking for the unicorn.

When the tailor heard a crashing sound, he turned to see the unicorn running straight for him. The tailor stood perfectly still. Just as the unicorn reached him, the tailor jumped out of the way. He had been standing in front of a tree. The unicorn's horn drove deep into the tree and became stuck in the hard wood.

The tailor freed the unicorn and rode it back to the palace in a cloud of dust. Again the king was amazed to see the tailor.

The tailor told the king, "For one who has killed seven in one blow, a unicorn is like a kitten!"

The king had no choice but to keep his promise. He thought his new son-in-law was a hero. He did not know that the man who married his daughter and took half his kingdom was a simple tailor.

Demeter and Persephone

Adapted by Megan Musgrave
Illustrated by Mike Jaroszko

Hades, the king of the Underworld, sat on his lonely throne one day and wished that something could make his world a nicer place to live. The Underworld was cold and dark and dreary, and the sun never shined there. No one ever came to visit Hades because the gates of the Underworld were guarded by Cerberus, a huge, three-headed dog. Cerberus looked so fierce that he scared everyone away.

It made Hades very grumpy to be the king of such a cold and lonely world. "I need a companion who will bring joy to this dark place," said Hades. He decided to disguise himself as a poor traveler and go up to the earth's surface. He would find someone who could help him make the Underworld a happier place to live.

Upon the earth lived Demeter, the goddess of the harvest. Demeter had a beautiful daughter named Persephone. Persephone had long, golden hair and rosy cheeks, and happiness followed her wherever she went. Demeter loved her daughter very much, and she was always full of joy when Persephone was near.

When the goddess of the harvest was happy, the whole world bloomed with life. The fields and orchards were always full of crops to be harvested.

Persephone loved to run through the fields and help Demeter gather food for the people of the earth. But best of all, Persephone loved to play in the apple orchards. There, she could climb the apple trees and pick large, juicy apples to eat.

One day when Hades was visiting the earth, he saw Persephone playing in an apple orchard. He had never seen such a beautiful girl. He stood at the edge of the orchard and watched her while she swung on the branches of the trees.

Finally, Persephone saw Hades standing nearby. In his tattered cloak, he looked like a poor and hungry traveler. Persephone was always generous, so she picked several large apples from the tree and climbed down to meet him. "Please," said Persephone, "take these apples. They will keep you from being hungry on your journey."

Hades thanked Persephone for the apples and went on his way. "I must bring her to the Underworld!" he thought to himself. "It could never be a gloomy place with such a kind and beautiful queen as this!" Then Hades returned to the Underworld.

The next morning, Persephone decided to pick some apples for her mother. She ran to her favorite orchard and began picking the ripest apples she could find.

Suddenly there was a great rumble, and the ground split open before her! Out from below the earth charged two fierce, black horses pulling a dark chariot behind them. On the chariot rode Hades, wearing the black armor of the Underworld.

Persephone tried to run away, but Hades was too quick for her. He caught her and took her away with him in his chariot to the Underworld. The ground closed back up behind them. Not a trace of Persephone was to be seen except a few of the apples she left behind.

When Demeter came home from the fields, Persephone was nowhere to be seen. Demeter went to the orchard where Persephone had been picking apples, and found some apples spilled on the ground. "Something terrible has happened to Persephone!" cried Demeter. She ran to search for her beautiful daughter.

After looking everywhere for her daughter, Demeter decided to visit Helios, the god of the sun. "Helios sees everything that happens on earth. He will help me find Persephone," she said. She went to the great castle of the sun, where Helios was preparing for the end of the day.

"I have seen Persephone," Helios said sadly. He told Demeter that Hades had taken Persephone to the Underworld to be his queen.

"The Underworld!" exclaimed Demeter. She knew how unhappy Persephone would be there. Demeter became very sad and lonely for her daughter. The earth became cold and snowy, and the crops in the field faded and died.

In the Underworld, Persephone was sad and lonely, too. She tried to make her new home a more beautiful place, but nothing helped. The ground was too cold to plant seeds, and there was no sunshine to help them grow. Finally she asked Hades to let her return to the earth.

"But you are the queen of the Underworld!" exclaimed Hades. "Not many girls have the chance to be a queen. I am sure you will be happy here if you only stay a while longer."

Persephone eventually became friends with Cerberus. Although he looked ferocious, he was lonely just like her. Sometimes he walked with her through the gloomy caves of the Underworld.

But even with her new friend, Persephone missed the sunny days and lush fields where she had played on the earth.

Demeter missed her daughter more and more with each passing day. Finally she traveled to Mount Olympus, the home of the gods. She asked Zeus, the most powerful god of all, for his help.

"Hades has kidnapped my daughter Persephone and taken her to the Underworld to be his queen! Please help me bring her back to earth again!" begged Demeter.

Zeus saw that the earth had become cold and barren. He knew that he had to help Demeter so that the earth could become fruitful again. "I will ask Hades to return Persephone," said Zeus sternly. "But if she has eaten any food in the Underworld, I may not be able to help her. Anyone who eats the food of the dead belongs forever to Hades." With that, Zeus took his lightning bolt in hand and traveled to the Underworld.

"Hades!" thundered Zeus when he reached the gates of the Underworld. He made his way inside easily, for even fierce Cerberus was afraid of the king of the gods.

Zeus found Hades sitting sadly on his dark throne, watching Persephone. Persephone hardly looked like the beautiful girl she had been before. Her golden hair had grown dull, and her rosy cheeks were pale.

"Hades, I demand that you return Persephone to the earth. Demeter misses her terribly, and the earth has grown fruitless and barren since you stole her daughter away," said Zeus.

"Very well," sighed Hades. "I thought her beauty would make my Underworld a happier place, but she is only sad and silent since she has come. You may take her back to the earth."

But Hades was very clever. He did not want to lose his queen, so he decided to trick Zeus. When Zeus was getting ready to take Persephone back to earth, Hades took her aside for a moment. He told her she would need food for her journey. He offered her a pomegranate, a large fruit which has juicy seeds to eat. Persephone ate just six pomegranate seeds before she returned to earth. But the pomegranate came from the Underworld. Persephone did not know that Hades had tricked her into eating the food of the dead.

Persephone said good-bye to Cerberus, and Zeus carried her back to the earth and her mother. When Persephone returned, Demeter was overjoyed. She was so happy to be reunited with her daughter that the earth bloomed again, and the crops came back to life. Demeter and Persephone planned to return to their happy life, harvesting good food for the people of the world. But their troubles weren't over yet.

Suddenly, Hades appeared before Demeter and Persephone. "Wait!" he exclaimed. "Persephone has eaten the food of the dead! She ate six seeds from a pomegranate before she came back to earth. She must live in the Underworld forever!"

Demeter and Persephone were upset that Hades had tricked them. Demeter did not want to give up her daughter again. One more time, she asked Zeus for his help.

Zeus was angry about the trick Hades had played, too. He thought very carefully before he decided that Persephone would not have to return to Hades forever.

"But," he said, "you did eat six pomegranate seeds. For each seed that you ate, you will spend one month of the year in the Underworld. The other six months you will spend here on earth with Demeter."

And so each year when Persephone returns to the Underworld, Demeter becomes very sad and lonely for her daughter. Winter comes to the earth, and it is cold and barren. But when Persephone returns to play in the fields with her mother, Demeter is overjoyed. The earth is fruitful and green, and summer reigns until Persephone returns to Hades again.

Gulliver's Travels

Adapted by Brian Conway
Illustrated by Karen Stormer Brooks

Gulliver was a doctor in the city of London. He grew tired of the crowded city, though, and decided to take a trip on a ship. He wanted to journey to distant lands and see many different people and things. He had no idea his voyage would take him to strange places that can't be found on any maps. This is the story of the little land of Lilliput, the first stop in Gulliver's many travels.

Sailing through the East Indies, the ship hit a terrible storm. Gulliver and five other sailors had to leave the sinking ship behind. They climbed into a small boat and dropped it into the stormy sea. At the mercy of the violent waves, the boat twisted and turned until suddenly it flipped over. The men tried to swim against the waves, but the water swallowed up Gulliver and his shipmates.

Gulliver awoke on a grassy shore. He could not move, but he thought he felt something moving steadily up his leg to his chest. He shifted his blurry eyes to see what seemed to be a tiny human being who was not much bigger than a spoon.

When he felt many more of these little people marching up his leg, Gulliver tried to lift his head. His hair, he found, was tied down, and his arms and legs were tied down, too. He struggled to lift one arm, breaking the tiny strings that bound it to the ground. Then he broke the strings near his head, making it easier for him to examine his surroundings.

He saw hundreds of the tiny creatures staring back at him. Some ran away from this massive human, while others shot arrows the size of needles at his free hand. Gulliver stayed still until he heard one little man talking to him in a language he could not understand.

Gulliver politely agreed with everything the little man said. This man must be their emperor, Gulliver thought. The emperor spoke kindly for the most part, and Gulliver did nothing to upset the small creatures. He did lift his hand again, however, to point to his mouth.

The emperor understood that he was hungry. He ordered basket upon basket of breads and meats to be carried up to Gulliver's mouth and dropped in.

Then the emperor pointed off into the distance and called for a cart that 500 tiny carpenters had built. The small creatures untied him. Gulliver cooperatively climbed onto the cart and allowed them to chain him to it. Then 900 of their strongest men pulled him to their capital city.

They tugged Gulliver to their largest building, an ancient temple just outside the magnificent little city. There they bound him in chains at the ankles. Gulliver understood their fear and their need to protect themselves from being trampled. He did not mind the chains too much, and he felt honored to stay in their temple. He could crawl in and lay down with only his feet sticking out.

Now Gulliver was eager, as always, to learn about this place and its tiny people. He crouched down to the ground and made every effort to speak with them. The emperor sent the finest scholars in the land to visit with Gulliver every day for several weeks. Soon, Gulliver learned that the curious kingdom was called Lilliput, and its gentle, intelligent people were known as Lilliputians.

The first words Gulliver learned to say to the Lilliputians were, "Please remove my chains." They told him it would take some time to remove them, and Gulliver understood well. They fed him regularly, after all, and he had no complaints.

Before too long the Lilliputians were no longer afraid of Gulliver. They fondly called him "The Man-Mountain" and came to see him often. They let Gulliver pick them up in his hand. That way, he could talk to them without crouching.

He showed them his coins and his pen, which they studied with great curiosity. The Lilliputians were especially amazed with Gulliver's pocket watch. Its ticking was very noisy to them, but they had many questions about how it worked.

Even the children of Lilliput came to love Gulliver. They would dance on his hand and play hide-and-seek in his hair. Gulliver enjoyed amusing the children. He wondered what he could do to entertain the other Lilliputians.

One day the army of Lilliput marched out to a field to practice its drills. The Lilliputians were very proud of their army, and Gulliver himself was fascinated with the soldiers' skill. Gulliver built a stage for their exercises. He used his handkerchief and several sticks to build the playing field.

He picked up 24 horses and 24 soldiers and put them on the stage. Then he lifted the emperor and his court in his hand so they could see the maneuvers from above. They liked this very much. So much, in fact, the emperor ordered that this entertainment be performed daily for everyone.

Then the day came when Gulliver would be released from his chains. But first Gulliver had to pledge an oath to the emperor. He stood before the emperor in the position that the law required, then he gladly made the promises they asked him to make.

"The Man-Mountain" promised to be forever careful where he walked. He agreed to deliver the emperor's important messages over great distances in little time. And he offered to help the Lilliputian army in times of war.

In return, the Lilliputians gave Gulliver his freedom and agreed to give him as much food as he could eat.

A few weeks later, the emperor visited Gulliver. He told Gulliver that the Lilliputians were getting ready for a battle. For many hundreds of years, the emperor explained, the Lilliputians had been at war with the only other kingdom they knew, an island nation called Blefuscu.

Long ago, Gulliver was told, the emperor of Lilliput and the emperor of Blefuscu had an argument over which end of an egg is best to crack first.

"It is only logical to break the egg on the larger end!" shouted the emperor of Blefescu.

"Only idiots would break the egg on the larger end! It is only logical to break the egg on the smaller end, of course!" the emperor of Lilliput shouted back.

That argument became a war that had never ended, and Blefuscu was now sending a large fleet of ships to attack Lilliput. The emperor asked for Gulliver's help.

Gulliver's job was to stop Blefuscu's ships before they reached the shores of Lilliput. He asked for several strong cables and a set of iron bars. Gulliver bent the bars into hooks and tied them to the cables.

The sea between the two kingdoms was much too deep for tiny humans, but Gulliver could walk easily through the water in very little time. He set out on his own across the sea.

Gulliver soon met the enemy ships as they left the shores of Blefuscu. He rose from the water and frightened the Blefuscudians terribly. Most of them dove from their ships at the sight of him and swam back to shore.

Some brave Blefuscudians stayed on their ships to shoot arrows at their giant foe. When Gulliver attached the hooks to their ships and started to pull them away, though, even the most fearless soldiers leaped from their ships to the water below.

Gulliver tugged the ships back to Lilliput. Great cheers rose from the shore as he came closer, holding the entire fleet of Blefuscu in one of his massive hands.

"Long live the emperor of Lilliput!" cried Gulliver.

From that day forward, the little people of Lilliput called Gulliver their greatest warrior of all time, because he alone ended many sad years of battle.

Having reached a peace with the Lilliputians, the people of Blefuscu invited Gulliver to visit their island. "The Man-Mountain" was happy to oblige them. He did not want them to be afraid of him, and he knew he had much to learn about their customs.

Gulliver spent two fine days on the island of Blefuscu. On the third day, while he took a walk on the beach, Gulliver spotted an empty boat in the sea. It was a real boat for a man his size!

Gulliver hurried to thank the Blefuscudians for their kindness, then he rowed the boat back to Lilliput to bid his dear friends a fond farewell. The emperor presented him with several live cows and plenty of food for his journey. Then Gulliver sailed away.

Before long, Gulliver spotted a ship like the one he had once sailed on. He rowed swiftly to it and was welcomed aboard. He told the crew about his voyage to Lilliput. No one believed his story until he reached into his pocket and pulled out the tiny cattle he had received from the emperor. That was more than enough to convince them.

Soon Gulliver was back in London, where people came to see his tiny animals. There he prepared for his next incredible voyage.

Ali Baba

Adapted by Brian Conway
Illustrated by Anthony Lewis

In a town in Persia there lived a man called Ali Baba. He was a poor woodcutter, and he struggled greatly each day to feed his wife and children. All he ever wanted was to own a shop in the town, sell goods to his neighbors, and have plenty for his family.

One day Ali Baba was cutting wood in the forest. He saw a troop of men on horseback approaching. Ali Baba thought these men were robbers, so he climbed a tree to hide.

Ali Baba counted 40 men. He wondered whether this could be the band of Forty Thieves he had heard so much about, the robbers that all of Persia feared. Their leader dismounted and stepped around a bush toward a large rock wall. The powerful man faced the wall, and Ali Baba clearly heard him shout, "Open, sesame!"

A door opened in the rock wall, revealing a secret opening to a cave. The leader stepped in, and the other robbers followed him.

Ali Baba waited until the thieves filed out from the cave. Their Captain closed the door, saying, "Shut, sesame!" Then the thieves rode away.

When he was sure they were gone, Ali Baba stepped toward the rock, as the Captain had done. Then he shouted, "Open, sesame!" And the door opened for him just as miraculously as it had for the Captain of Thieves.

Ali Baba stepped through the threshold to find a large room, filled at every inch with all sorts of valuables, so brilliant with gold, silver, and jewels that Ali Baba had to squint.

He feared the robbers might soon return. He hurriedly made a pouch with his cloak and gathered as much gold as he could carry. Ali Baba remembered in his haste to say, "Shut, sesame!" when he left the cave.

Ali Baba did not notice one small but important thing as he hurried away from the cave to share his fortune with his family. A single gold coin dropped from his cloak to the base of the bush that covered the secret door. Fortunately for Ali Baba, the thieves did not notice the coin that day, or the next day either, or for several days until a few weeks later.

The Captain of Thieves caught sight of the single coin's glimmer one day. He was very angry.

"How could you drop this and risk revealing our hiding place!?!" the Captain shouted at his 39 robbers.

"But, Master," the thieves told him meekly, "we know the punishment for such mistakes is most severe. Surely none of us has done this."

"Then we have been found out," the Captain growled. He paced for several minutes. Then he announced, "We must learn who is newly rich in the town. That man and all his family must die."

By now Ali Baba had opened the shop of which he'd always dreamed. He was a fair and generous shop owner. After all, he could afford it, with a pile of gold at home and more in the secret cave whenever he would need it. He was happy, his family had plenty, and every neighbor was his friend.

Ali Baba hired a helper named Morgiana. She was a very clever and beautiful young lady. She enjoyed her work at the shop. And Morgiana cared for Ali Baba and his family very much.

Then a stranger came calling at the shop one day. He asked Morgiana many questions about the owner, Ali Baba. The stranger's questions worried Morgiana. She vowed to keep a watchful eye on the shop.

The thief in disguise returned to the robbers' cave. "His name is Ali Baba, Captain," said the thief. "He lives behind his new shop in town. He was a poor woodcutter only a few weeks ago."

"Go back there at nightfall," the Captain ordered. "Mark the house with this white chalk, and later, I will take twenty men there and finish him."

As he was told, the thief crept in the shadows to mark Ali Baba's home. Little did he know that clever Morgiana had spotted him. She followed with white chalk, too, and marked all the shops.

When the Captain and his 20 thieves arrived later that night, they found every shop was marked. They did not know which shop to attack, so they crept away in shame.

Their leader was very angry. "Will somebody get this right, once and for all?" cried the Captain.

One brave thief stepped forward. "Here is some red chalk," the Captain offered. "Mark the shop again, and I will lead 30 men to storm Ali Baba's home and end this threat."

The thief did as he was told, but again Morgiana played her trick on the Captain and his 30 thieves.

The Captain decided to use all his power against Ali Baba. The Forty Thieves gathered together and made a plan. The Captain would disguise himself as an oil merchant. He would lead a train of mules that carried 39 barrels. The thieves would hide inside the barrels and await their Captain's signal. It seemed like an excellent plan.

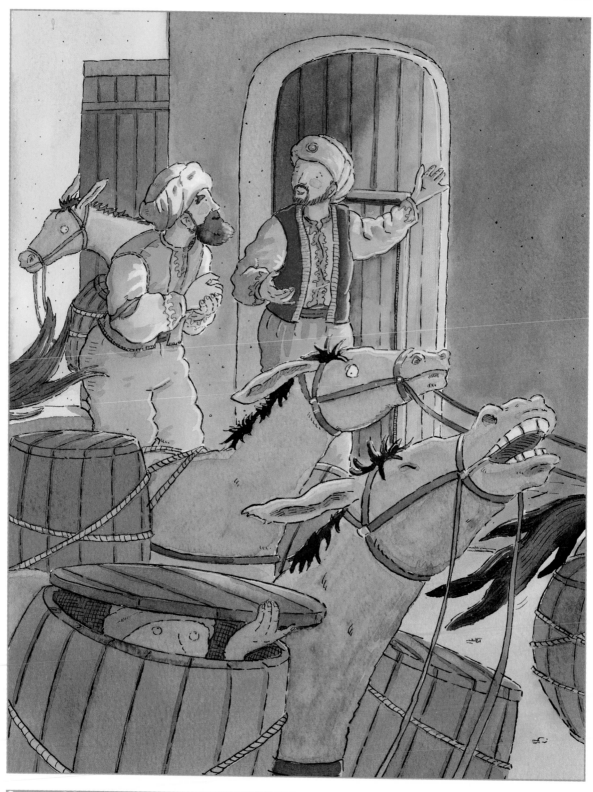

Early that night, they arrived at Ali Baba's shop.

"I have brought some oil to sell at market tomorrow," the Captain lied. "But tonight I need a place to stay. Will you take me in?"

Ali Baba was as generous as usual. "Of course you can stay here," he replied. "Leave your cargo in back. There is hay there for the mules. Then come in for dinner."

In the yard, the Captain whispered to his men, "Wait until you hear my signal. Then you must leave your barrels and storm the house."

Morgiana helped Ali Baba's family feed their guest. She thought it strange that a man would arrive so early for market, but the oil merchant seemed very polite.

After everyone had gone to bed, Morgiana finished cleaning up. Her lamp ran out of oil. She thought she'd have to finish cleaning in the dark until she remembered the many barrels of oil in the yard.

She walked up to the first barrel. A voice came through and whispered, "Is it time?"

Morgiana sensed danger. She answered, "Not yet, but soon." Then, gathering some hay around each barrel, Morgiana lit the hay with a torch. The 39 cowardly thieves coughed from the smoke. They popped out from their barrels and ran away to keep from getting burned.

Morgiana grinned as they ran off. Think of it! She alone had thwarted the infamous Forty Thieves not once, not twice, but three times!

The Captain of Thieves made his signal, but none of his men moved. He smelled the smoke then. Something had gone wrong again. He was not surprised. The Captain returned to the cave to find his 39 robbers. They were certain they'd be punished for running off, though, and each vowed the Captain would never see him again.

On his own, the single thief in the lonely cave decided he would have to use all his cunning to plan his revenge. It would take time, too, he knew.

He dressed carefully as a shop owner, went into town, and took up lodgings at an inn. He opened a shop across the road from Ali Baba's shop. The Captain lived as Cogia Hassan for many months. He waited in this disguise until precisely the right moment.

Ali Baba wanted to invite the newest shop owner over for dinner. He sent his son across the road with several gifts of friendship. Cogia Hassan graciously accepted the gifts but refused the invitation on many occasions.

After a full year had passed, the Captain at last agreed to dine with Ali Baba. He brought a basket of fine goods. He smiled as he met Ali Baba and his family, but he secretly carried a dagger in his cloak. The blade was intended for Ali Baba and his son.

Morgiana saw the dagger first. She thought Cogia Hassan had looked familiar, and now she knew why. He was the devious oil merchant who had threatened Ali Baba's household one long year ago.

Morgiana wished to save her beloved benefactors. She wore a headdress and several long, flowing silk scarves. She called for a servant to play music, then entered the dining room to dance for their guest.

Morgiana danced close to Cogia Hassan. She brushed him with a silk scarf. Stepping behind Cogia Hassan, Morgiana wrapped the scarf lightly around his arms then pulled hard. He could not move.

"What are you doing?" Ali Baba cried. "This man is our guest."

"This man is your enemy," she explained. "Would a friend bring a dagger to dinner? This man is the Captain of the Forty Thieves!"

At that, Ali Baba's son seized the dagger, and the Captain of Thieves was sent directly to prison.

"I owe you my life, Morgiana," Ali Baba said. "Please marry my son and join our family in name as well as deed."

Morgiana agreed. They celebrated a splendid wedding. Ali Baba told his son and Morgiana about the riches in the secret cave and the words that would open the door. All their children and their grandchildren were rich forevermore.

The Five Brothers

Adapted by Brian Conway
Illustrated by Leanne Mebust

Once upon a time there were Five Brothers who all looked exactly alike. They lived with their dear mother in a little house beside the sea. The family kept to itself in that fine little house. They took good care of each other, and they never needed to go to the village nearby. For five very good reasons, they never needed anyone's help at all.

These Five Brothers looked just like each other, but they were not like everybody else. Their father had been a sorcerer once, and somehow these Five Brothers came to have special abilities. They could do things that no one else in the whole world could do.

The First Brother could slurp up the whole sea and hold it in his mouth. His skill was most useful when it came time for fishing.

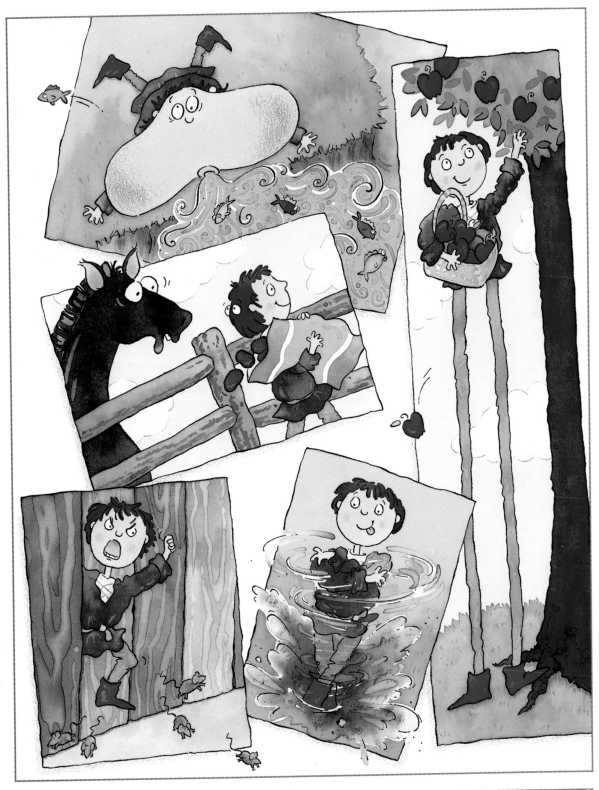

The Second Brother could see through the back of his head. This was helpful for finding animals when the brothers went hunting in the woods.

The Third Brother could creep through even the smallest cracks. He was a great help to his mother when he crept through the walls and scared away the mice.

The Fourth Brother could stretch and stretch and stretch his legs. He could reach the finest fruit in the tallest trees.

The Fifth Brother could spin like a top, only faster. When he spun around, the Fifth Brother could spin into the ground just as deeply as needed to dig a fresh well.

When fishing day came, the First Brother, who could swallow the sea, set out with his brothers. He stood on the shore, leaned over, and slurped up the whole sea in his mouth. He could not hold the water very long, so his brothers hurried to gather the largest and finest fish for their mother.

Now it happened that, at that very moment, the king was having a swim in the sea just up the shore. The king liked complete privacy when he bathed. He had extremely large feet, you see, which he took great efforts to hide from the villagers.

With the water suddenly gone from the sea, however, the king's funny feet were laid bare for all the village to see.

"Who has taken the water away?" the king shouted to his guards. "Go and find him!"

Well, the Five Brothers gathered a few fish that morning until suddenly they heard angry cries coming from the village. Then they saw soldiers quickly approaching them. The First Brother tried to put the water back in its place just as quickly as he could, while his four brothers hurried home with their fish.

"Who do you think you are, taking all of the sea for yourself?" the king scolded. "You have made a fool of me, and you will be punished for it!"

The king decided the First Brother would be quickly banished from the kingdom. He ordered the guards to blindfold him, take him deep into the woods, and leave him there.

"Please, Your Highness," said the First Brother, "allow me to go and bid my dear mother good-bye."

"It is only fair," the king agreed.

The First Brother went home and asked the Second Brother to go back in his place.

The guards covered the Second Brother's eyes. They led him for many miles through the woods, twisting and turning away from any paths, around tree after tree.

Then they left him in the forest to fend for himself.

The Second Brother, who could see through the back of his head, knew exactly where he was, and how to get back. He came out of the woods even before the guards did. Walking home, though, he met the guards. They grabbed him and brought him before their king.

"You are clever," said the king, "but I know what to do with you."

The king ordered the guards to lock the Second Brother inside a box and carry him by buggy to another kingdom.

"Please, Your Highness," the Second Brother pleaded, "allow me to go and bid my dear mother good-bye."

"It is only fair," said the king.

The Second Brother went home and asked the Third Brother to go back in his place.

The Third Brother, who could creep through any crack, was locked in a box. Two soldiers lifted the box onto a buggy. They watched the buggy roll away down the road. They turned to go back to the castle and report the good news to the king, but standing right there behind them was the Third Brother! They grabbed him and brought him before their king.

"So you are more clever than I thought," growled the king. "I know what to do with you."

He ordered the guards to take the Third Brother out to sea, and drop him in the deepest waters.

"Please, Your Highness," the Third Brother pleaded, "allow me to go and bid my dear mother good-bye."

"It is only fair," said the king.

The Third Brother went home and asked the Fourth Brother to go back in his place.

The guards took the Fourth Brother aboard a boat. They sailed to the deepest waters and dropped him in. The Fourth Brother, who could stretch and stretch and stretch his legs, did just that until his feet could touch the bottom of the sea.

The guards stayed for most of a full day to watch him sink. The Fourth Brother did not sink. He happily stared back at them, his head bobbing up and down on the crest of the waves. Finally the guards pulled him out of the water and brought him before their king.

The king was very angry. "Take him to the dungeon and leave him there! He'll get no food or water!" the king shouted. "I never want to see him again!"

"Please, Your Highness," the Fourth Brother pleaded, "just let me go and bid my dear mother good-bye."

"I suppose it is only fair," said the king.

The Fourth Brother went home and asked the Fifth Brother to go back in his place.

The guards led the Fifth Brother to the cold, lonely dungeon of the king's castle. They threw him in among four hard stone walls and a solid stone floor.

"You'll get no food or water," the guards told him scornfully. "No one will ever see you again."

With that the guards slammed the thick stone door and sealed it shut.

Now the Fifth Brother, who could spin faster than a top, knew there was nothing below him but more solid rock. He could not dig, as he had done so many times for his mother.

"I shall spin in the other direction," the Fifth Brother decided. "Then I will go up."

The Fifth Brother turned and turned, spinning to a blur. He raised his arms from his sides and flew up, up, up through the roof above him.

The king was in his chamber, getting ready for bed, when the floor began to rumble.

Alarmed, the king jumped up on his bed as the Fifth Brother came spinning up through the floor!

"H-h-how did you...?" the angry king stuttered. "You are more than clever. You are a demon!"

He reached for his blade and called for his guards.

"Please, Your Highness," the Fifth Brother pleaded. "I am different, it is true. I have a gift, just like you."

"What do you mean?" the curious king asked.

"Your grand feet can be used for a very important job in the kingdom, Your Highness. Making mashed potatoes!" the Fifth Brother replied.

And so the king came to know that he, too, could do things that no one else in the whole world could do. He no longer felt foolish about his feet. He showed them off proudly each day as he walked barefoot through his kingdom.

Every day the king made enough mashed potatoes to feed the entire kingdom, and the Five Brothers shared their finest fish, meat, and fruit with all the king's subjects. Everyone in the kingdom had plenty, and many found they had gifts they never knew they had before. The Five Brothers and their mother became the most trusted and respected family in the land as they enjoyed a lifetime supply of mashed potatoes.